300
FIRST WORDS

Introduced by BETTY ROOT

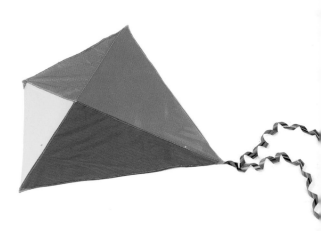

Photographed by GEOFF DANN

BARRON'S

About this book

There is no doubt that the right books help to develop children's language. Young children love sharing a book with a grown-up, identifying familiar objects and talking about them, and this book is designed to help them do just that:

– its size is right for a small child
– the photographs are colorful and clear
– the picture grouping extends the child's range of interest
– the words are all common ones
– the objects shown are familiar and can easily be identified with the real thing
– the animals are both domestic and wild.

At first, toddlers will enjoy simply looking for the pictures you name and pointing to them. With just four pictures on each double-page spread, answering questions such as "Where is the tea pot?" or "Which one do you sleep in?" is easy for them when there are only four choices. Getting the answer right is very important to young children. It builds their confidence and encourages them to take their next big step, which is telling you the names of things. Sometimes they will compare the photograph in the book with the actual object, and this may lead to lively discussion about similarities and differences.

Later on, children will enjoy puzzling out less direct questions: "What tells you the time?" "Which do you put on your feet?" "Which do you ride?" If they answer correctly, you will know they really understand the word. Now you can encourage them to reverse roles and ask you the questions.

Gradually, they will begin to understand that the printed squiggles they see under each picture are written-down words and later on, as their early reading skills start to develop, the book will help them to identify words beginning with particular sounds.

Above all, *300 First Words* is designed to make learning fun!

Betty Root

baby

rattle

baby's bottle

bib

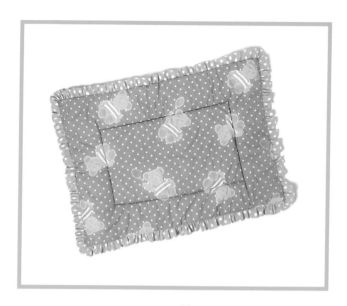

quilt

crib

stroller

carriage

hairbrush

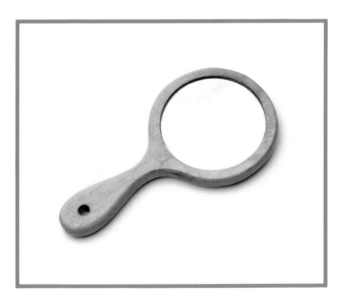

mirror

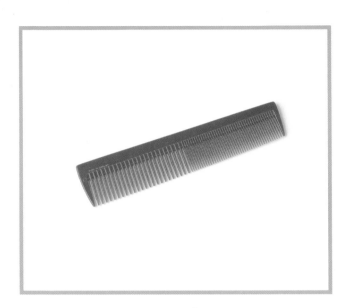

comb

hair dryer

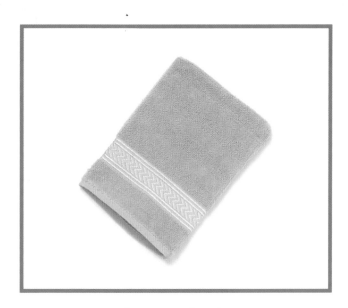

facecloth

soap

towel

shampoo

sponge

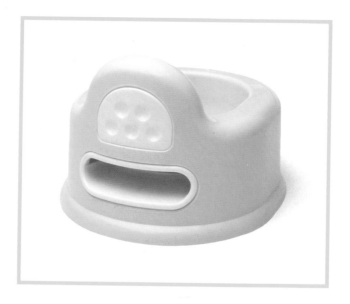

potty

toothbrush

toothpaste

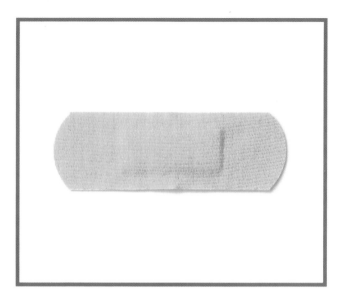

Band-Aid

cotton balls

nail scissors

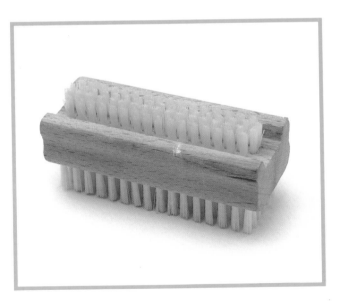

nailbrush

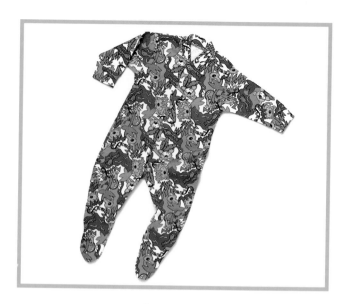

sleeper

pajamas

bathrobe

slipper

undershirt

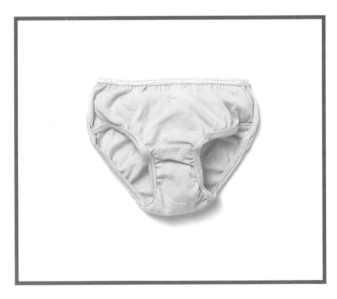

underpants

sock

shoe

shirt

pants

belt

overalls

T-shirt

shorts

cardigan

dress

sweatshirt

skirt

scarf

sweater

wool hat

glove

mitten

jacket

rain hat

raincoat

umbrella

boot

bathing suit

sandal

sun hat

sunglasses

bucket

shovel

paddle

ball

teddy bear

doll

penguin

Jack-in-the-box

picture book

alphabet block

jigsaw puzzle

shape-sorter

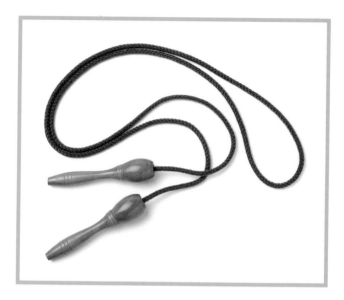

jump rope

tricycle

balloon

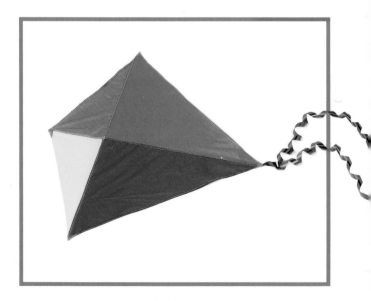

kite

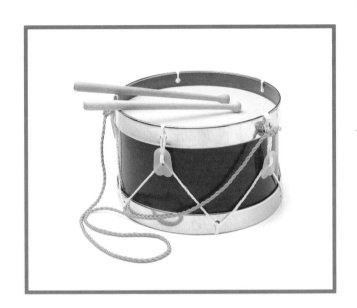

drum

tambourine

trumpet

recorder

guitar

violin

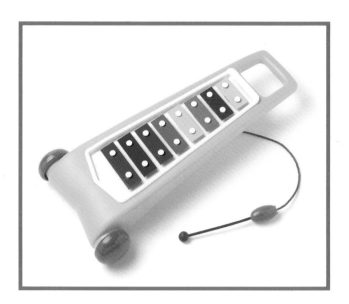

xylophone

triangle

crayon

felt-tip pen

paintbrush

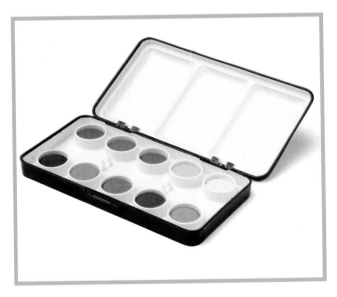

paint box

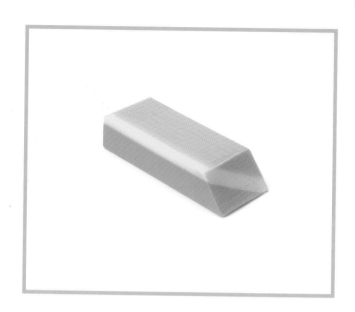

eraser

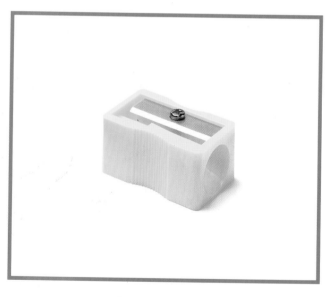

sharpener

pencil

pencil case

wallet

basket

knapsack

suitcase

glasses

flashlight

pocketknife

watch

bracelet

ring

necklace

earring

apple

orange

lemon

pear

banana

grapes

pineapple

peach

tangerine

melon

strawberry

apricot

tomato

cucumber

lettuce

carrot

peas

corn

broccoli

cauliflower

potato

cabbage

avocado

onion

ice cream

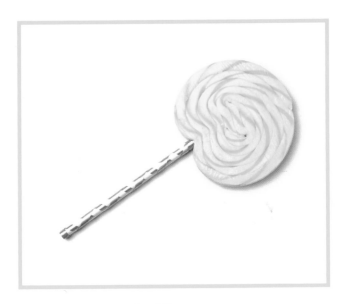

lollipop

chocolate

cake

cookie

bread

sandwich

roll

butter

cheese

egg

spaghetti

honey

jam

orange juice

milk

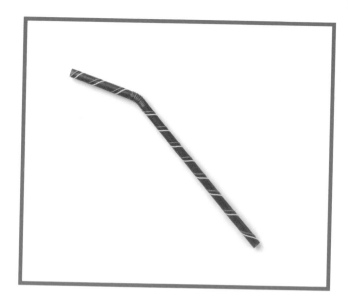

straw

glass

baby cup

mug

cup

saucer

bowl

plate

knife

fork

spoon

egg cup

pitcher

tea pot

kettle

coffee pot

wooden spoon

colander

frying pan

pot

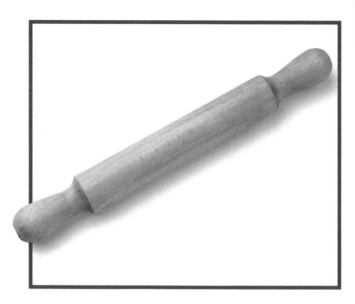

rolling pin

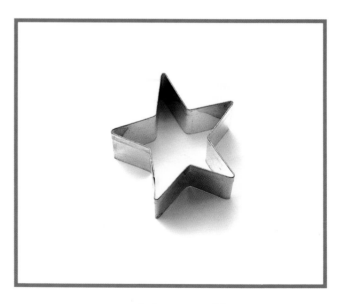

cookie cutter

cake pan

oven mitt

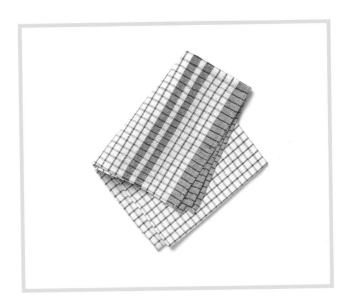

dish towel

mixing bowl

sink

rubber glove

pepper grinder

salt shaker

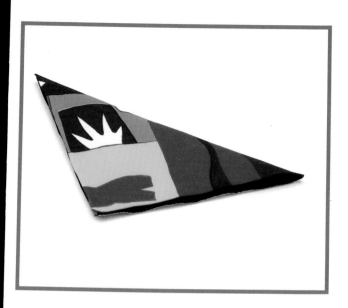

napkin

table

chair

desk

armchair

sofa

telephone

calculator

clock

picture

television

computer

radio

camera

pillow

bed

sheet

blanket

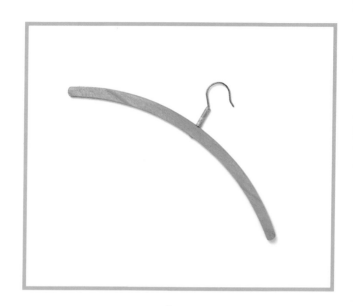

coat hanger

wardrobe

cupboard

dresser

light bulb

lamp

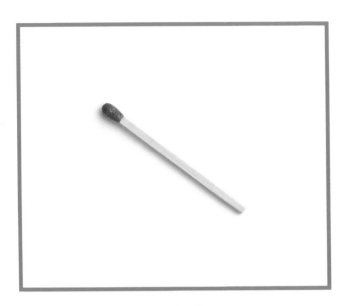

match

candle

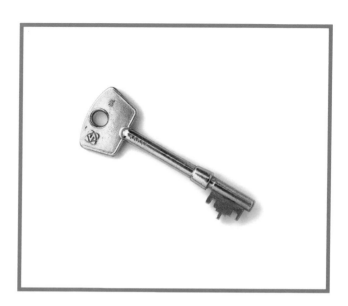

key

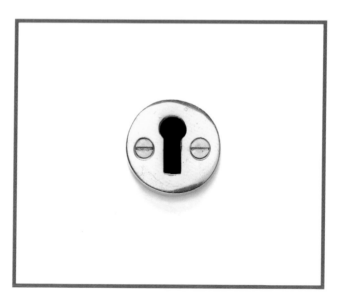

keyhole

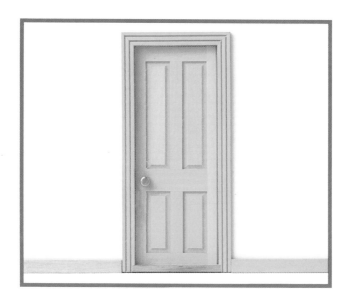

door

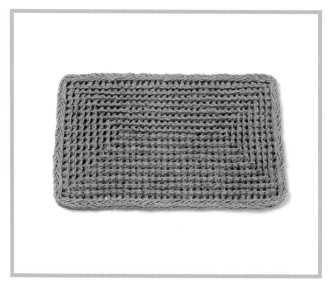

doormat

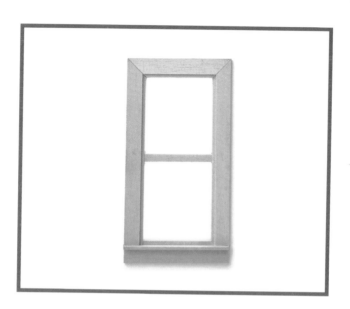

window

curtains

vase

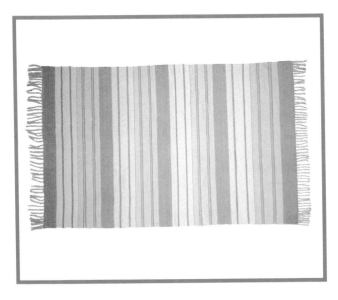

rug

broom

vacuum cleaner

brush

dustpan

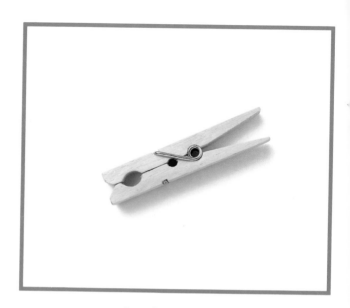

clothes pin

laundry basket

iron

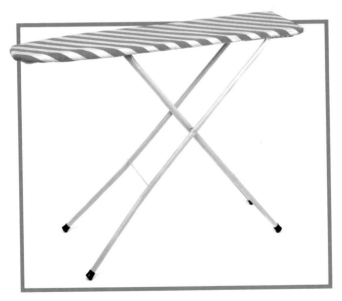

ironing board

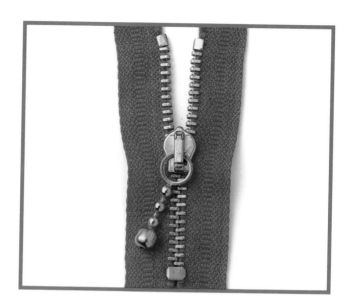

zipper

buckle

bead

button

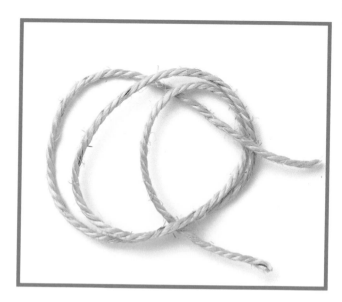

string

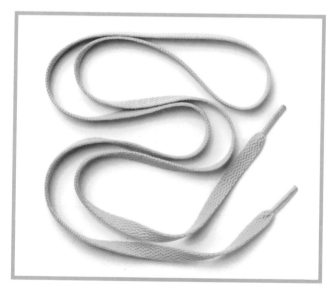

shoelace

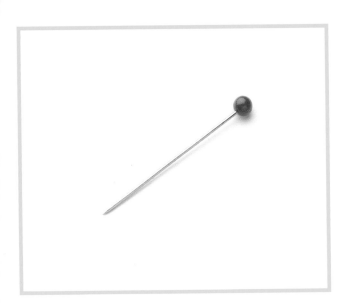

pin

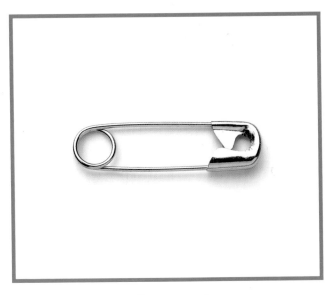

safety pin

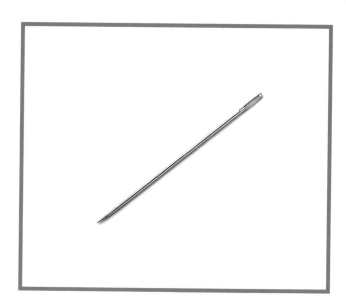

needle

thread

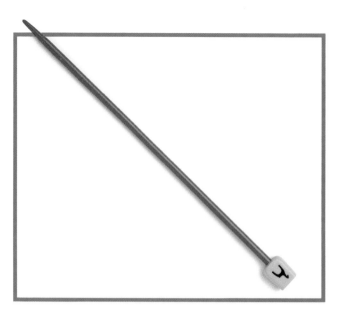

knitting needle

yarn

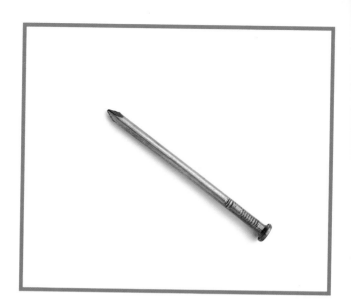

nail

hammer

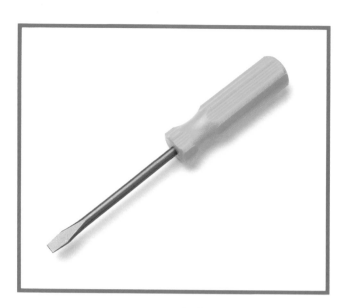

screwdriver

screw

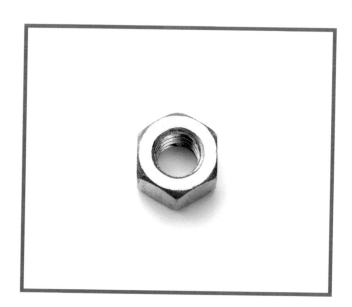

nut

wrench

pliers

saw

garden fork

trowel

watering can

flowerpot

grass

soil

leaf

plant

rose

tulip

iris

geranium

butterfly

dragonfly

ant

spider

cat

dog

horse

cow

hen

rooster

goat

sheep

donkey

pig

goose

duck

lion

tiger

giraffe

panda

zebra

camel

rhinoceros

elephant

bear

reindeer

ostrich

kangaroo

turtle

crocodile

dolphin

whale

fish

starfish

crab

seashell

tractor

combine

excavator

bulldozer

crane

truck

146

car

wheel

motorcycle

crash helmet

bicycle

bell

helicopter

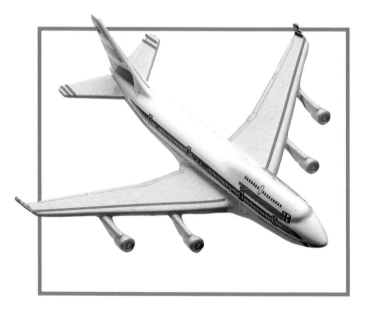

airplane

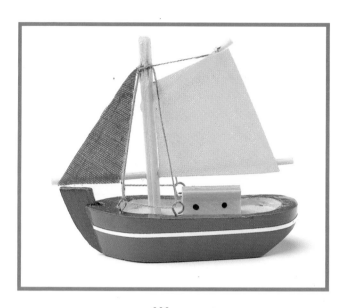

sailboat

speed boat

postcard

package

birthday card

envelope

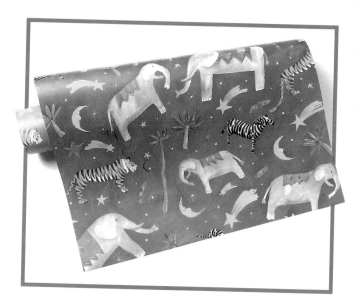

wrapping paper

ribbon

bow

present

Index

First U.S. edition published in 1993 by Barron's Educational Series, Inc.

Text copyright © Frances Lincoln Limited 1993
Photographs copyright © Geoff Dann 1993

Published by arrangement with Père Castor-Flammarion, Paris

Doll's furniture by courtesy of Rainbow, 253 Archway Road, London N6 5BS
and The Singing Tree, 69 New King's Road, London SW6 4SQ

All inquiries should be addressed to:
Barron's Educational Series, Inc.
250 Wireless Boulevard
Hauppauge, New York 11788

Library of Congress Catalog Card No. 92-44750

International Standard Book No. 0-8120-6356-2

Library of Congress Cataloging-in-Publication Data
Dann, Geoff.
   300 first words / introduced by Betty Root : photographed by Geoff
Dann. — 1st U.S. ed.
     p.   cm.
   Summary: Labeled pictures introduce basic vocabulary words.
   ISBN 0-8120-6356-2
   1. Vocabulary—Juvenile literature. [1. Vocabulary.] I. Title. II. Title:
Three hundred first words.
PE1449.D277   1993
428.1—dc20

                                              92-44750
                                              CIP
                                              AC

PRINTED IN HONG KONG